SKELETONS IN YOUR CLOSET

A Book for Christian Families
About How Human Life Began

By Dr. Gary E. and Mary M. Parker

Illustrated by Jonathan Chong

Master Books

SKELETONS IN YOUR CLOSET
First printing May 1998

DEDICATIONS

Diane David Deborah Dana Mary Gary

TO OUR CHILDREN'S CHILDREN: GINA RUTH, BRIAN PAUL-MICHAEL, RENEE MARIE, TYLER EDWARD, SAMANTHA LYNN, MALCOLM LEVI, PRESTON DAVE, AND THOSE YET TO COME: "REMEMBER NOW THY CREATOR IN THE DAYS OF THY YOUTH..." (ECCL 12:1A).

Jonathan Jodia Jasmine Jacinthe

THIS BOOK IS DEDICATED TO MY FAMILY. GOD HAS BLESSED ME RICHLY THROUGH ALL OF YOU.

JONATHON CHONG
ILLUSTRATOR

CHAPTER 1
"CAVEMEN" AND OTHER PEOPLE

Have you ever wondered what "cave men" were like? Did God create people, or did apes change into people without God's help? How do bones of apes and people turn into fossils? What do those fossil skeletons tell us about how people began?

The Bible tells us that God created people with a plan and purpose, each one in His image and gave them earth as their perfect and peaceful home. But people became selfish and turned against God in sin. Sin brought struggle and death into the world, and God's judgement at the time of Noah's flood.

The flood, and disasters that followed it, turned the bones of many animals and people into fossils — "skeletons in the closet" of human history, you might say. But the best news in the Bible is this: Jesus Christ came to die for our sins and to give us new life now, and life forever in heaven with God! God created, man ruined, Jesus brings new life — that's the Bible's message.

Sad to say, however, not everyone believes God's Word. Textbooks, teachers, television, magazines, movies, and museums often tell a very different story of human beginnings, a story called "evolution." According to evolution, time and chance somehow made "dead" stuff come to life. Then struggle and death made some apes change into people — but people and all living things finally die out or become extinct.

The Bible and evolution are really exact opposites. The Bible says that God created man, that man's sin brought death, and that Jesus, God's Son, brings new life. Evolution says that struggle and death created many, that man made up one idea of God, and man and all life finally dies.

Which is it? Is the Bible true, and life wins? Or is evolution true and death wins? What do science and Scripture really tell us about those fossil skeletons in the human closet? Were there ever any "ape-men?" Are "cave men" mentioned in the Bible?

I'm Dr. Gary Parker, a Christian and a scientist. My wife, Mary, and I have special training and experience in the study of fossils. Our four children, Dana, Debbie, David, and Diane, like to hunt for fossil skeletons with us.

Our children love to ask questions, too. Don't be surprised if some of your questions, like our daughter Debbie's, begin with a science discussion at school.

Deb: Boy, Dad, I'm mad.

Dad: Why, Deb?

Deb: Today our class went on a trip to the museum to see the skeletons of people and animals that lived in the past.

Dad: You mean fossils?

Deb: Yes. In this one room they had skeletons and models of "cave men."

Dad: Neanderthals (Nee AN der talls)?

Deb: Yes. That's what they were called — Neanderthals.

Mom: Sounds like an interesting trip. What made you so mad?

Deb: You know those Neanderthals living in caves? In the museum they were all bent over and very hairy. They looked sort of like apes.

Neanderthal
MAN

6

Mom: I know. I've seen that museum display myself.

Dad: That same picture shows up in a lot of my science textbooks, too.

Deb: Well, I told my teacher I thought that display wasn't right. I told her — nicely, of course — that the Bible and science tell us that God made people as a special creation, directly from materials in the "dust of the ground."

Mom: That's what the Bible says all right. And since God, who was there, doesn't tell lies, we can be sure that's exactly what happened. What did you teacher say about that?

Deb: At first she just sort of smiled at me. Then she said that some people do believe that God created man's spirit, but science has proven that man's body has evolved from the apes.

Mom: Oh?

Deb: And then some kid piped up and said that God must be a pretty bad designer. Just look at how bent over our cave man ancestors were!

ADAM **OR** CREATION
APE-MAN EVOLUTION?

Dad: I can see why you might have gotten a little upset.

Deb: A *little* upset! Then someone else — a friend of mine no less — said if God made people out of dust, He must be busy making a whole tribe out of the dust under his bed. That's when I really got mad!

Mom: What did you do?

Deb: Well . . . nothing. I didn't know what to do. When Dad explained how God shaped people from the atoms of the ground, it all seemed so real — especially how God designed us to think, to plan, and to love one another, just like He loves us.

Mom: All that is true, Debbie.

Deb: If all that is true, where do "cave men," like those Neanderthals, fit in? Were those museum models and skeletons just fakes?

Dad: Those *skeletons* weren't fakes, Deb. In fact, scientists have discovered many fossil skeletons of Neanderthals, several nearly complete. The first were discovered in Germany over 100 years ago. They have also been found in France and Israel and other places.

Deb: Well, why were the Neanderthals so hairy? Isn't that sort of half ape, half man?

Dad: Wait a minute, Deb! Remember your cousin, Tom? He has lots of hair on his body. Does that make him less human than your cousin Jim, who hardly even needs to shave?

Deb: Now I remember the Bible's description of Jacob and Esau, too. One was a "hairy man" and one was a "smooth man," but they were equally human — twin brothers in fact!

Esau and Jacob

Mom: In Burma back in the 1800's, a girl was born with hair all over her body, in a pattern sort of like a wolf's. Her name was Krao Farini. Newspapers, which love to exaggerate, called her part ape, and published pictures of her to "prove it."

Dad: She was actually a very intelligent girl, who mastered three languages as she grew up. Her condition shows up now and again — but it never makes a child less human! Human beings have lots of skin pits that form hair, and sometimes pits that usually form "peach fuzz" hair form bigger, thicker hairs instead.

Krao Farini

Mom: Besides that, Deb, the hair on the museum models really is "fake" in a way. The remains we have of Neanderthal cave men are mostly just fossils of their bones.

Deb: I see what you mean, Mom. You couldn't really tell from the bones whether the living person had hair or not, or where the hair was, or how much.

Dad: That's true of the fleshy part, too, like the soft parts of the ears and nose and shape of the face.

Deb: Come to think of it, the models gave the Neanderthal faces very broad, flat noses and very thick lips. Was that just fake, Dad?

Dad: Let's put it this way, Deb, the artist who made the model could just as easily have given the Neanderthals lips and noses with different shapes.

Deb: So, since you can't tell what the soft parts really looked like, you can make them as much like a human or like an ape as you want. Think how a Hollywood make-up artist can make the same actor look like a handsome man or a monster.

Dad: *Creation* magazine once interviewed an artist who was hired to draw Neanderthals. He was simply told to make them look ape-like.[1] Medical experts can compare skulls with features of living people, so they don't have to just guess or make up faces like evolution believers do.

Mom: Remember the fossil camel skull we found in Kansas? A picture in *Creation* magazine showed how it could be drawn to look like a vicious meat-eater even though we know it's a gentle plant eater[2].

Dad: In that sense, the fleshed-out museum model doesn't really tell us about the Neanderthals. It just tells us about the *artist's belief* about them — the artist's own prejudice or bias.

Camel Skull   Reference

Deb: It sounds to me as if Neanderthal faces could be just like those of ordinary people. But why were the models all hunched over?

Mom: Remember how straight and tall your grandfather was until he got hunchback from injury and disease?

Deb: Yes, I remember. Maybe Neanderthals had bone diseases.

Dad: That they did, Deb. The biggest problems were lack of vitamin D and iodine in the Neanderthal's diet, but they had other bone diseases as well.

Mom: Evolution believers thought bent over Neanderthals were *apes on their way up* to becoming man, but science showed the Christians were right: the first Neanderthals found were bent over people on their way down from bone diseases!

Deb: Good one, Mom. Besides, Grandma says her bones ache when the weather gets cold and damp. Isn't it cold and damp in caves? Maybe living in caves made Neanderthal bone diseases even worse.

Dad: You're probably right, Deb. Good thinking.

Deb: Why did Neanderthals live in caves anyway? I guess that means they were pretty dumb.

Dad: Not at all. In fact, we have a lot of evidence that cave people were smart!

Deb: Oh? What kind of evidence is that?

Dad: Their cave paintings, for example, are very good (much better than a lot of "modern art," I'd say!). Some could even make their drawings look 3-D.

Mom: The way they buried their dead shows that they believed in heaven, or at least in life after death.

Dad: And that takes a sense of purpose and meaning, plus abstract thought, language, and a grasp of eternity — being able to think about "forever." Just like the Bible says, God put eternity into people's minds (Eccl. 3:11).

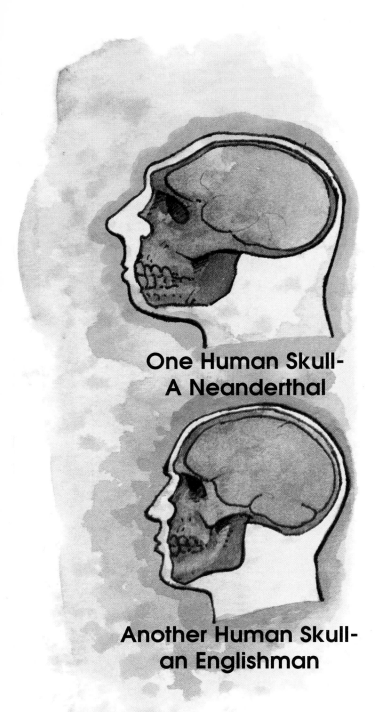

**One Human Skull–
A Neanderthal**

**Another Human Skull–
an Englishman**

Deb: But what about the shapes and sizes of their heads? The skeletons and museum models showed big ridges over their eyes and sloping foreheads. Does that mean they had small brains?

Dad: Not at all. In fact, most Neanderthal cave men had brains *bigger* than the average for most people living today!

Mom: Besides that, people with lots of different brain sizes all have the same intelligence. After all, the average size of a woman's brain is slightly less than a man's, but women are just as smart.

Deb: I should say so! But what about their living in caves? Does that mean anything?

Dad: Did you see any models or skeletons at the museum of "cave people" called Cro-Magnon (Cro MAN yon)?

Deb: Yes. They stood quite straight and tall, both men and women.

Dad: The Cro-Magnon people stood straighter and taller and had higher foreheads than most people living today. Did the museum display show where they were living?

Deb: Yes, it did. They were living in caves, just like the Neanderthals. Come to think of it, I guess that means you can be tall, smart, and handsome and still live in a cave!

Mom: Dressed up in modern clothes, Neanderthals would look pretty handsome, too. In fact, there's a museum in Germany that took its wax model of a normal Neanderthal man (without bone diseases) and dressed him up in a business suit, just to show he could walk right down Main Street and nobody would notice anything unusual! The museum didn't want people to be fooled any more into thinking Neanderthals were half ape, half human.

Deb: That's great, Mom and Dad! Now I know what I'm going to say if someone asks me where cave people fit into the Bible.

Mom: What's that, Debbie?

Deb: I'm just going to say, "Cave people were just people who lived in caves!"

Dad: An excellent point, Deb. And you know what? Except for a couple with really poor arguments, modern scientists agree with you. Neanderthals are now given the same scientific names as you and I, *Homo sapiens*.

Mom: That happens over and over again, Debbie. When all the facts are in, science supports the Bible and proves evolution is wrong.

Deb: Are cave people mentioned in the Bible?

Dad: In a way they are, Deb. David, the shepherd and psalm-writer who became king of Israel, spent a lot of time living in caves when he was fleeing from Saul.

Deb: What about Stone Age cave men. When did they live?

Dad: Actually, Debbie, there are Stone "Age" people living on earth *right now*. The so-called "Stone Age" does *not* tell us *when* a people lived; it only tells us what kind of *tools* they used.

Mom: Some evolution believers use the term Stone "Age" because they want to make us think there was a *time* in the past when *all* people were "primitive," that is, only a little smarter than apes but not as smart as people today.

Dad: But science proved evolution wrong once again. In the past or present, we may find some peoples at some times and some places using only simple, "*primitive*" *tools*, but *we **never** find "primitive" people*!

Deb: But what about the Tasaday people I read about in *National Geographic*?

Dad: Those were just modern people *pretending* to be Stone "Age" to fool *National Geographic*, and it worked — just like other "experts" in human evolution have been fooled in the past.[3]

Deb: Come to think of it, there are a lot of tribes in the world today who use stone tools. And they are people created in God's image, just like we are.

Dad: Right you are, Debbie. In fact, many respond to missionaries and become Christians and Christian teachers! And people from any culture can be taught to fly airplanes, write books, compose music, or do anything else so-called "modern" people can do.

Deb: One thing for sure, using stone tools or living in a cave doesn't make a person less a person!

Mom: That's true, Debbie. All people were created as part of God's family, and Jesus died and rose to bring them back into fellowship with their Creator, *Jesus Christ, the God of all peoples, all times, and all places.*

Deb: That means each person in the whole wide world is very special to God.

Dad: Amen, Deb. Amen.

CHAPTER 2
FROM ADAM AND EVE TO ME

Believers in evolution now admit it was very wrong to say cave people, like Neanderthals, were ape-men. Even more sadly, evolution once regarded other peoples as part ape and part human, especially those with different skin colors.

What does the Bible have to say about the many varieties of people living on earth? Could all people have come from just the two people, Adam and Eve, whom God created in the beginning? Join our conversation with Debbie again, and let's discover the answer together.

Deb: Why didn't the museum tell us the whole truth about Neanderthals? The museum display made cave people look stupid and ape-like. Why didn't they tell us about the bone diseases, and about their large brains, and about their art and beliefs?

Mom: I'm afraid the sad truth might be something like this, Deb. That museum display wasn't trying to teach you science; it was trying to teach you evolution instead.

F A L S E

Neanderthal Man

Just plain Human
Homo-sapiens

Dad: People who believe in evolution believe apes changed into people, and they have been looking for fossil skeletons that would show some creatures part ape and part man — "ape-men," as they're often called. We've just been talking about the most famous of the so-called "ape-men," the Neanderthal cave people.

Deb: But Neanderthals aren't half-ape and half-man! They're 100% human! Cave people are just ordinary people who lived in caves.

Dad: You're absolutely right, Deb. Everybody knows that now. That's why the link between ape and man which evolution believers hope to find is often called the "missing link."

Mom: We now know that Neanderthals are fully human, not part ape or sub-human. But, very sadly, Neanderthals are not the only people once claimed to be sub-human "missing links" by those who believe in evolution.

Deb: Really? You mean there are other people once thought to be part ape?

Mom: It wasn't long ago when that view of evolution was taught as "fact." Here's a big newspaper article from the 1920's that your grandfather kept.

Deb: Hmmm. This article is about the Bushmen in Australia. Did evolution believers once call Australian Bushmen sub-human missing links?

Dad: It's sad, but true, Deb. There's a really terrible bit of history about the last survivors among the natives on Tasmania, the southern island state of Australia. The settlers believed so strongly that the Tasmanian natives were part animal that they formed a human chain across parts of the island to hunt down and kill all the native peoples.

Mom: Later, when the last surviving native, an old woman named Truganini, was about to die, she begged to be buried with her people, not sent off to a museum.

Deb: You mean somebody wanted to put her on display in a museum, just like a passenger pigeon or some other extinct animal? What happened?

Mom: She died, and they shipped her off to a museum. That's how strong the belief in that kind of evolution was before World War II.

Dad: Evolution even played a role in World War II.

Deb: Really? How's that?

Dad: The war was started by the Nazi leader, Hitler. Evolution is based on constant struggle to the death among different "races" or varieties. Hitler believed some people were superior to others, and had the right to kill off other "races" in a struggle for survival.

Bushmen Are Missing Links

Deb: Ugh! How awful!

Mom: Perhaps the saddest story of evolution going against both science and Scripture involves the black people of Africa. Back in the 1920's, a famous scientist who believed in evolution wrote that "Blacks" belonged to a different species than "Whites."

Dad: Even worse, he wrote that the average adult of the "Black species" was no smarter than an eleven-year-old child of the "White or human species."

Deb: Is that a terrible joke, Daddy? Do you mean people like Jim, my friend from school who comes over to work on math with me . . . or Sandra on the cheer squad with me . . . or Jamie in our church choir — do you mean evolution believers once thought people with black skin weren't really human at all? How horrible! Didn't that "famous scientist" have any black friends?

Mom: It does seem that his belief in evolution blinded that scientist to some simple, everyday facts — and to some important facts of science as well.

Dad: The good news is that most people who believe in evolution today now agree with what the Bible was teaching all along: Bushmen, Blacks, and everyone else are just plain people.

Mom: The Bible has always had it right: God made of one blood all the tribes, languages, and nations of people that dwell on the earth, just as Paul preached to the Greeks (Acts 17:26).

ADAM & EVE

Dad: Remember, Deb, science is <u>not</u> the enemy of the Christian faith; science is the Christian's friend in the fight against evolution.

Deb: That is good news! But you know . . . I have wondered about something. Since all people started from just Adam and Eve, where did all the other people come from? The Bible says Adam and Eve had three sons, Cain, Abel, and Seth, and Cain killed Abel. Who did Cain and Seth marry?

Mom: The Bible also says that Adam and Eve had other sons *and daughters* (Genesis 5:4). So, at the very beginning, brothers must have married sisters.

Deb: Yuk! That sounds terrible! Besides, I heard that if you marry a close relative, you'll have weird children!

Dad: Today, it is unwise to marry a close relative, Debbie, because we all carry mistakes in our bodies called mutations. These mistakes cause birth defects and disease.

Deb: Where did these mistakes come from? I thought God created our world perfect.

Mom: God did create us and our world perfect. But mankind's sin and selfishness ruined God's world. So, until Jesus comes the second time and makes the world perfect again, we have to live with death, disease, disaster — and those mistakes called mutations.

THEIR CHILDREN

NATIONS OF PEOPLE

22

Where did Cain get his wife?

Cain could marry his sister!

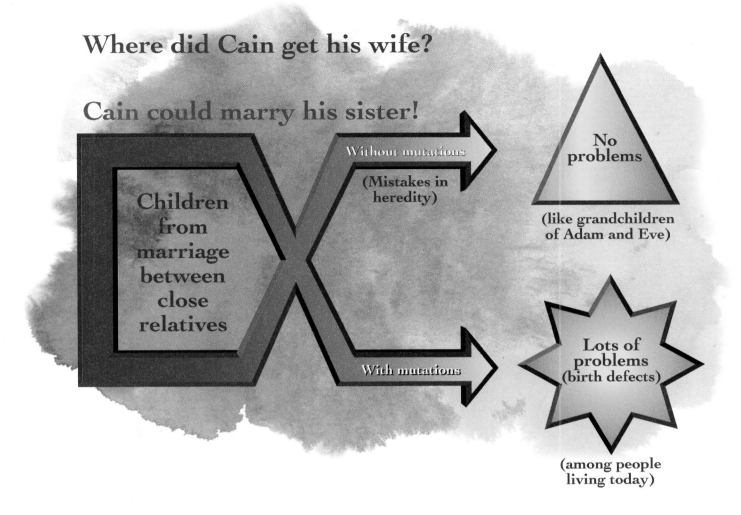

Children from marriage between close relatives

Without mutations
(Mistakes in heredity)

With mutations

No problems
(like grandchildren of Adam and Eve)

Lots of problems (birth defects)
(among people living today)

Deb: What about Adam and Eve? Did they have these mistakes?

Dad: Not before they sinned or rebelled against God. After that, mistakes began to build up in their children and grandchildren. That's why many generations after Adam and Eve, God told Moses to write a law against marrying close relatives.

Mom: Usually it's only when both parents carry the same mistake that their children may have a problem, and that's more likely to happen if both parents are closely related.

Deb: I think I see now. Cain, Seth, and other sons of Adam and Eve could marry their sisters because their bodies carried few or no mistakes. But mistakes have been getting worse and worse since sin ruined our world, so God doesn't want us to marry close relatives today.

Mom: Excellent, Deb. By the way, though, never let anyone tell you Cain married a woman from the "Land of Nod." In the Bible, "land of Nod" just means "land of wandering."

Dad: Even science traces all human beings back to just two people. The Bible calls them Adam and Eve, and all of us came from just those two and no others.

We all have the same skin color
MELANIN

AABB   AABb   AaBb   Aabb   aabb

Just different amounts of it!

Deb: That makes me think of something else, Dad. Since we all came from just two people, how did human beings get so many skin colors?

Dad: The answer may surprise you. There's just <u>one</u> skin color. Every person with skin color has the <u>same</u> skin color.

Deb: How can that be? Some of my friends look a lot darker than others, and you're a lot darker than Mom and I!

Dad: Even so, Deb, there's just one thing that gives everyone their skin color. It's a protein called melanin (MELL ah ninn). You and Mom have a little of it. Jonathan and Jodia, our Chinese friends, and I have more, and one member of our family, Levi, has the most anyone can have. So, in that sense, we all have the same skin color — just different amounts of it.

Deb: Clever, Dad. But tell me, since God created just two people at the start, how long did it take to get all the different amounts of skin color people have today?

Dad: The answer could be just one generation — certainly not a million years, nor a thousand years, but just one generation.

Deb: Really? You mean the children of Adam and Eve could have been just as dark or just as light as anyone living today — and everything in-between?

Mom: That's right, Debbie. As you know, it's things called genes that control how tall we'll be, whether we'll have curly, straight, or wavy hair, how our bodies work, and other things like those.

Dad: Well, there are two main pairs of genes that control how much skin color we'll have. We can call them Aa and Bb. Look at this chart from one of my books, Debbie. It shows how those "color genes" mix together in different ways when people marry and have children.

Deb: Hmmmm. That's interesting. If a child gets four "big" genes (AABB), he or she has the darkest skin color. Four little genes (aabb) mean very light skin. And the rest of the brothers and sisters in that family could have any skin color in-between. That's neat!

Maximum Variation
AaBa x AaBa

	AB	Ab	aB	ab
AB	AA BB	AA Bb	Aa BB	Aa Bb
Ab	AA Bb	AA bb	Aa Bb	Aa bb
aB	Aa BB	Aa Bb	aa BB	aa Bb
ab	Aa Bb	Aa bb	aa BB	aa bb

Only Dark AABB   Only Medium aaBB   Only Light aabb

Dad: Parents with medium skin color and mixed genes (AaBb) are common in India today, Debbie. So, some people from India are as dark as the darkest African; some as light as any Swede; and most are in the middle.

Mom: We once knew people from India who showed all the shades of human skin color in just one family!

Deb: So that's why we have people that are mostly dark, light, medium, or mixed today! When people multiplied and spread out over the earth, they sorted out the colors God built into Adam and Eve right at the very beginning!

Mom: That's right, Deb. But things got a little more complicated after the Tower of Babel, when God broke people up into small groups with different languages.

Dad: If parents in one language group had only "big genes" (AABB), that's all they could pass on to their children, so . . .

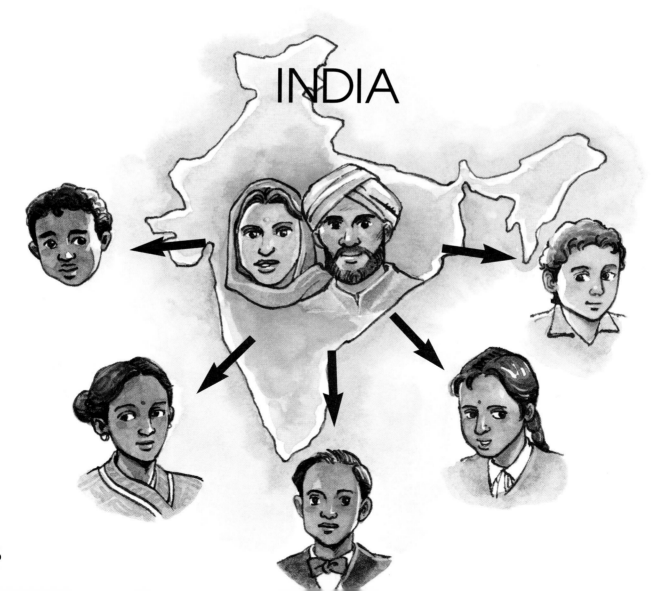

INDIA

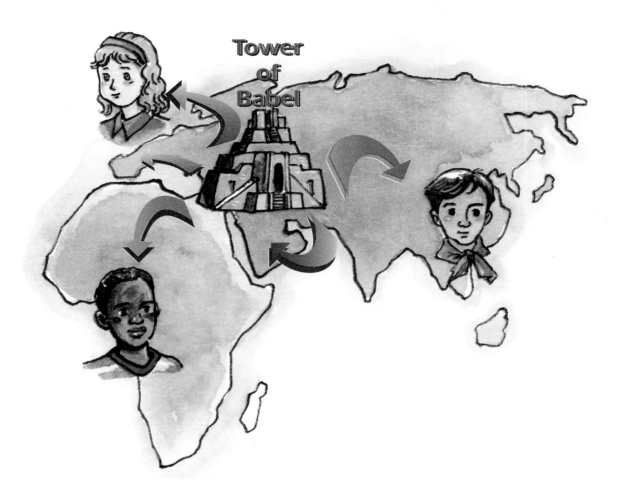

Deb: . . . So their children would all have very dark skin.

Dad: And if parents in another group had only "little genes" (aabb), that's all they could pass on, so . . .

Deb: . . . So their children would all have very light skin!

Mom: Excellent, Debbie, and parents with two big and two little genes of the same kind (AAbb or aaBB) would always have children with medium skin color, like Orientals, Polynesians, and your Dad's ancestors, the American Indians or Native Americans.

Dad: But parents with mixed genes (AaBb) can have children with any skin color, all according to the plan of God built into our first parents, Adam and Eve.

Deb: Thanks a lot for explaining all that, you two. I guess that proves that when God said He made of one blood all nations that live on earth, that's exactly what He meant! We all have the same great, great grandparents, Adam and Eve. And we all belong to the same family, the family created by God!

Dad: Amen, Debbie. And that's not all. Science tells us that God could build so much variation into just two people that Adam and Eve could have more children than there are sand grains by the seashore or stars in the universe without having any two children (except twins!) exactly alike!

Deb: Wow, Dad. I like the song that says "God made me special; I'm the only one of my kind." I guess that's really true!

Mom: It is indeed, Debbie. In fact, nobody in the past ever had your combination of traits, and nobody in the future ever will. You have a special place in God's plan that nobody else can take – and that's true for each child conceived and every baby born!

Dad: Don't you wish each person knew how special he or she is in God's plan?

Deb: I surely do, Dad. I guess that's one reason it's so important to tell everyone about Jesus, and about how important they are to Him, and how He can give joy and purpose to their lives, and a place with Him in heaven forever.

CHAPTER 3
MISSING LINKS ARE STILL MISSING!

In spite of all the mistakes evolution believers have made in the past, some people still believe in evolution. In fact, some dig up fossil bones and teeth, hoping to find some sort of skeleton in our closet that would look like a link between ape and man. That's what science fiction movies and some science textbooks call "the search for the missing link." As we shall see, lots of fossil bones and teeth have been dug up, and lots of tall tales told, but the missing links are still missing.

Our son, David, heard things in school that made him ask us some important questions about these so-called missing links. When it comes to human beginnings, the science classroom can be a pretty exciting place!

Dave: Dad, I shared some of the things you told Debbie about cave people with my class at school.

Dad: Oh? What happened?

Dave: The teacher agreed with you on Neanderthal and Cro-Magnon. He said, just like you did, that cave people were just ordinary people—*Homo sapiens*—like you and I. But then he said there are lots of other fossils that do show how apes changed themselves into people. Is that true, Dad?

Dad: Well, let's find out. Let's pack a picnic lunch and take off for the museum. We'll take a look first hand at those skeletons in the human closet. We'll see what they really tell us about human beginnings.

HOP ON YOUR IMAGINATION TRAIN AND TAKE THE MUSEUM TOUR WITH US. SEE IF YOU CAN DECIDE FOR YOURSELF WHERE THE EVIDENCE LEADS US: TO ADAM OR APE!

Dave: Boy, this museum looks like fun. There's the Neanderthal cave man display you and Debbie talked about.

Mom: Before scientists discovered Neanderthals were just people, evolution believers claimed these cave people were missing links that showed how apes changed into people. But science proved evolution wrong.

Dad: The next fossil skeleton claimed to be an ape-man was discovered in 1912, outside the village of Piltdown, England.

Dave: That must be the one called "Piltdown Man." I think I've heard of Piltdown Man before. Wasn't Piltdown Man a fake, a hoax, or something like that?

Mom: Yes it was, David. It's probably the most famous fake or fraud in the history of science.

Dad: A man named Dawson reported a large part of a skull and most of a lower jaw buried with a few stone tools and some animal fossils.

Piltdown
MAN

The world's human evolution experts agreed Piltdown is a link between apes and man — But the world's experts were fooled by a mistake!

Mom: In fact, experts from all over the world studied the Piltdown find. Almost all these experts agreed that Piltdown Man was a link between ape and man. They gave Piltdown the scientific name Eoanthropus (E AN thro puss), which means "dawn man."

Dave: But it turned out to be a fake, right? What was it really?

Dad: Really it was just a human skull, with a few key parts missing, and the jaw of an ape whose teeth had been filed. Both parts were stained to make them look older.

Dave: How did all those experts miss the stain and the file marks? I guess it must have been a really smart person who made up the Piltdown fake.

Dad: Strangely enough, the hoax was *not* that clever. When a scientist named Clark looked at the teeth over forty years after the fake was found, he said the file marks on the teeth were easy to see.

Mom: That's the real tragedy of the Piltdown hoax, David. It wasn't shown to be a fake for over forty years. For those forty years, it was hailed as "proof positive" that people evolved from apes.

Dad: In fact, when I was collecting fossils in Sweden in 1982, I found a museum that still listed Piltdown Man as evidence for evolution!

Mom: For over three generations of students, the message in schools was something like this: "You can believe the Bible if you want to, but the facts are all on the side of evolution."

Dave: And all the time the real facts were on the side of the Bible! Piltdown was just a plain fake, not even a very clever one at that!

Mom: Right you are, David.

Dave: I just thought of something else we can learn from Piltdown. Some of my friends at school said evolution must be true because all the experts believe it. But Piltdown proves that all the experts can be wrong, even about something as important as human beginnings!

Dad: In fact, it isn't the first time all the evolution experts have been wrong. They were wrong about Neanderthals, wrong about Blacks and Bushmen, and badly wrong about the Piltdown fake! In science, it's not the majority who are right, but the scientist who has the evidence to back up his theory.

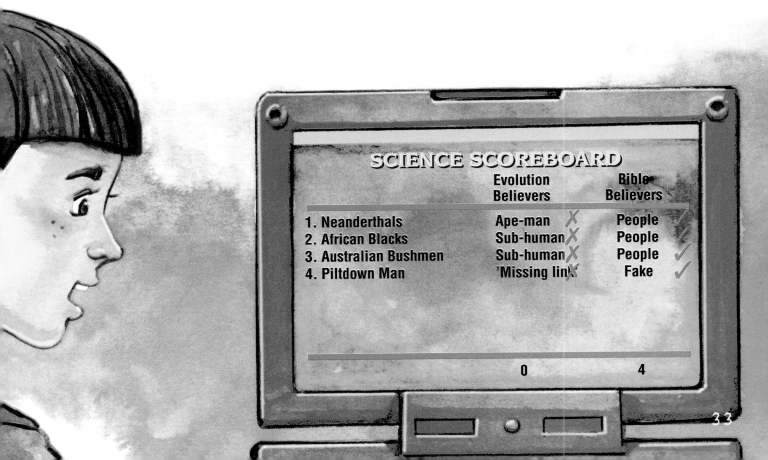

SCIENCE SCOREBOARD

	Evolution Believers	Bible Believers
1. Neanderthals	Ape-man ✗	People ✓
2. African Blacks	Sub-human ✗	People ✓
3. Australian Bushmen	Sub-human ✗	People ✓
4. Piltdown Man	'Missing link' ✗	Fake ✓
	0	4

Mom: Speaking of evidence, take a look at this display.

Dave: That's just the top of a skull and a leg bone. Is that supposed to be an ape-man?

Dad: Once it was. It was called "Java Man," and first given the scientific name *Pithecanthropus* (Pith e CAN thro puss).

Mom: You may as well get used to two big words, David. In Greek, "pithecus" (PITH e cuss) means "ape," and "anthropus" (AN thro puss) means "man."

Dad: Notice, Dave, the name first given to Java Man, *Pithecanthropus*, literally means "ape-man."

Dave: Boy, Dad, scientists surely use big words when little ones would do just fine!

Dad: Well, later on Java Man's name was changed to *Homo erectus* (Ho mo e REKT us). "Homo" is the little word in Latin for "man."

Dave: That's a little better. But what was Java Man, anyway—an ape, a man, or partly both?

JAVA MAN
Pithecanthropus
'ape-man'

Dad: Actually, Dave, Java Man was probably nothing at all. The bones were found over fifty feet apart in gravel. Gravel is made of broken-up rocks moved around by water, so there was never any reason to think the skull cap and leg bone came from the same individual.

Dave: That sounds a lot like another hoax, like the Piltdown fake, to me.

Dad: It wasn't a trick done on purpose to fool people, like Piltdown was, but it wasn't much better. A man named Dubois (Dew BWAH) discovered the separate pieces falsely called Java Man. But he also found regular human skulls in the same gravel.

Dave: Wait a minute, Dad! That would prove the Java fossils he found could *not* be the ancestors of people because people already existed!

Dad: Good thinking, Dave. Maybe that's why the finder didn't tell anyone for over thirty years about the human skulls he discovered.

Dave: That's not fair! Holding back the truth like that is almost the same as telling a lie!

Mom: At least Dubois finally told the truth, and no informed scientist calls the Java mistake an ape-man anymore.

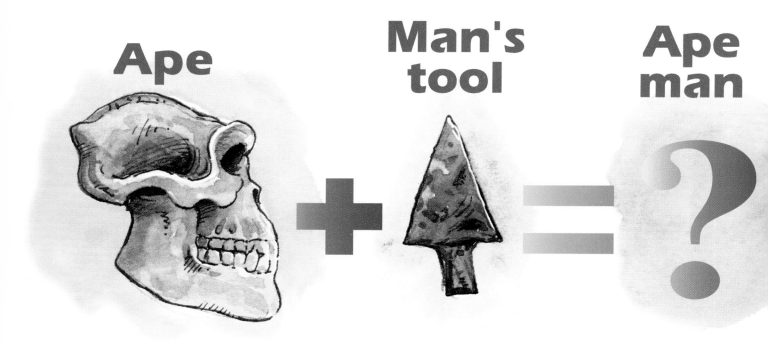

Ape + Man's tool = Ape man ?

Dave: Look at the next display. The skull has such a huge jaw that I can see why it was called "Nutcracker man." But the skull really looks more like a gorilla's than a man's. Is that one a fake or mistake, too?

Dad: Beliefs about so-called human evolution have been very embarrassing for science, Dave. Sorry to say, Nutcracker Man looks like another huge mistake.

Mom: The skull fragments were found by Louis and Mary Leakey in Africa. Their discovery got them the support of *National Geographic*, and made them famous.

Dave: I hear about the Leakeys a lot from my teachers. They seem like "evolution heroes."

Mom: The Leakeys and other evolution believers all agreed that the size and shape of the skull was very clearly ape-like. But the skull was found buried with evidence of human tools.

Dad: So, evolution believers proclaimed the "owners" of those gorilla-like skulls were the ones who made the tools. Ape skulls plus human tools equal a tool-using ape, an ape-man missing link—so they said.

Dave: That doesn't sound like such good evidence to me. Maybe the human tools were used <u>on</u> the ape skulls, not <u>by</u> the apes.

Mom: A nice bit of detective work, David. Many scientists now agree with you. In fact, there are still tribes of people who like to eat the brains of apes.

Dad: Monkey meat is too tough and stringy to eat. But if you lop off the heads of the apes and boil them up, then you can bash in the skulls, and eat out the goody—"monkey brains on the half shell," you might say.

Dave: Yuk! How disgusting!

Dad: At any rate, thirteen years after his parents found the gorilla-like skulls buried with human tools, Richard Leakey found bones like those of modern man buried deeper. That means people were already living, dying, and being buried before their so-called ape-man ancestors.

Mom: In other words, David, Nutcracker Man was just an ape who might have been man's meal; he could never have been man's ancestor.

Dave: Why are things like the Java and Nutcracker mistakes still pictured in museums and science textbooks? They're even taught as proof for evolution. Isn't that really lying to people who visit museums—and lying to children in school?

Mom: It may be just plain ignorance, David. When someone claims they've found a missing link, it makes all the headlines. But nobody carries the story later, when the claim is proven false.

Dad: A while back, a famous news magazine carried a big cover story on human evolution. It started by making fun of the Bible. Then, it said, the facts began to roll in for evolution: Neanderthal Man, Java Man, etc.

Dave: But all those so-called facts are wrong! Neanderthals were just people; the Java finds were nothing; and the Nutcracker fossils were probably just apes eaten by people! The Piltdown fake would be evidence just as good for evolution as those things!

Dad: That's the point, Dave. Those false claims for evolution got newspaper headlines. But nobody told the newspapers or news magazines about the scientists who proved those claims were wrong!

Mom: Unfortunately, there have been other huge mistakes. One bone, once claimed to be an ape-man, turned out to be an alligator's upper leg bone. Another was a horse's toe bone. One was a dolphin rib—although the evolutionist who found it thought he could prove it was an ape-man who walked upright!

Dad: In the United States, the most famous mistake was the fossil evidence for "Nebraska Man" and his family—all made up from a single tooth!

Dave: How could anyone make a picture of a family from a tooth?

Mom: No one really can, Dave. But there was even a famous court battle between evolution and the Bible, called the "Scopes trial." At that time (1925), a famous evolution believer convinced many news reporters and some scientists that the Nebraska tooth proved evolution.

Dad: But two years after those stories about Nebraska Man, an identical tooth was found with its real skull attached to its real skeleton. It wasn't the tooth of a man, or an ape, or an ape-man at all.

Dave: What was it?

Dad: It was the tooth of a pig.

Dave: A PIG! A pig's tooth was once called man's ancestor?! Boy, Mom and Dad, I didn't know scientists could make mistakes <u>that</u> big!

Mom: Remember, Dave, scientists are just human beings, and anyone can make a mistake. Still, those trying hard to prove human evolution have made far bigger mistakes than scientists usually do.

RAMAPITHECUS

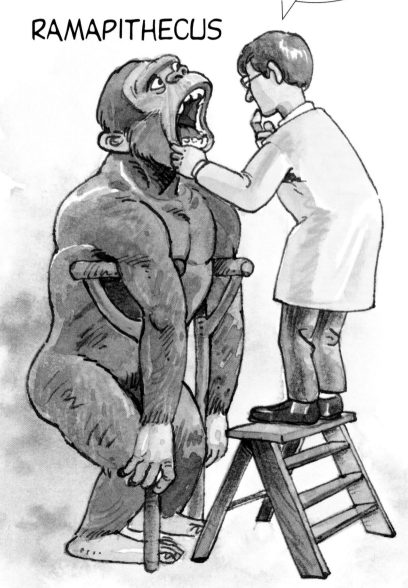

I THINK IT WALKED UPRIGHT.

Dad: Dave, I hate to tell you this — because it's an embarrassment to all scientists — but there is another case almost as bad as Nebraska Man.

Dave: Oh no! What's that?

Dad: *Ramapithecus* (RAH mah PITH ee cuss). We'll just call it Rama for short.

Dave: What's so special about Rama?

Mom: Did you see those tote bags in the museum gift shop?

Dave: The ones that are supposed to show evolution from bent over apes, to apes standing up, to people?

Mom: Those are the ones. Well, *Ramapithecus* was supposed to be the first ape that walked upright, on two legs.

Dave: How did they know Rama walked upright?

Dad: That's the bad news, Dave. The first fossils found of Rama were just pieces of jaws and teeth.

Dave: Jaws and teeth! How could you tell from jaws and teeth that Rama walked on two legs?

Dad: You can't, Dave. But when just a few fragments of jaw were found, evolution believers tried to make them fit into a curve about half way between the curve of a human's jaw and an ape's jaw.

Mom: But then scientists found the whole jaw, and proved Rama was just an ape after all.

Dave: It sounds to me like a little evidence can be used to support evolution, but more evidence and the rest of the story supports the Bible!

Dad: I agree, Dave. But I think the *least* evidence used to support evolution was the tooth that was *not* there.

Dave: What do you mean, Dad?

Dad: Well, *Discover* magazine did a cover story on a jaw that had the canine teeth — the pointed ones — missing. But the hole where they would have been was small. So, said an evolution believer, the pointed teeth must have been small . . . which means they could not have been used as weapons . . . which means the animal must have had its hands free to hold weapons. . . which proves it must have walked upright!

Dave: You've got to be kidding, Dad! That's not even good science fiction, let alone good science!

THESE BONES OBVIOUSLY BELONG TO A FEMALE 'APE-WOMAN' WITH AN I.Q. OF 47 WHO WAS CARRYING ONE OF HER 3 CHILDREN AS SHE WALKED UPRIGHT.

Dad: I certainly agree with you, Dave. But even Rama was only dropped as a "false start to the human parade" in 1979 — over fifty years after the lesson should have been learned from the pig's tooth called Nebraska Man.

Mom: Even today, Rama is still pictured in textbooks, magazines, and on museum tote bags — even though scientists now know that picture is completely false.

Dave: You know, I just noticed something, Mom and Dad. It seems like science is always proving evolution wrong. Where did the idea of evolution ever come from, anyway?

Dad: It did **NOT** come from the study of fossils, that's for sure! In fact, **evolution is really not science** at all. It's a belief about the past — a belief made up by men who weren't there, men who don't know everything, men who have certainly made some huge mistakes about the past already!

Dave: I know evolution believers have made some really big mistakes about fossils in the past. But I learned about evolution in science class. Why did you say evolution was really not science?

Dad: Look at this fossil I had in my pocket, Dave. When does that fossil exist — past or present?

Dave: Don't be silly, Dad. That fossil exists right now, in the present. Otherwise we wouldn't be able to see it.

Dad: So, when people dig up fossils, are they digging up the past or the present?

Dave: Hmmm. Really they are just digging up bits and pieces of bone found in the present.

Mom: So, when an evolution believer tells you this tooth belonged to an ape-man who walked upright and had several wives who lived in caves while he hunted — is that science?

Dave: Of course not! That's just his story about what might have happened in the past.

Mom: Was anyone there to see what really happened?

Dave: No. And our science teacher told us science only works on things we can see or measure and that other people have to see and check our measurements. Now I see what you mean: evolution is just storytelling; it's not science at all.

Dad: That's right, Dave. To study the past, we have to use the methods used in history, not in science.

Mom: And, David, what's the best kind of evidence a student of history can find?

Dave: In history, people really want most to find a written record that tells them what really did happen in the past.

Mom: And what does the Christian have in God's Holy Word, the Bible?

Dave: Wow, Mom and Dad! The Bible is like a history book for the whole universe! God was there, and He tells us what really did happen in the past — and God never tells lies or makes mistakes like human "experts!"

The Bible is the "history book of life," written by the one who was there—

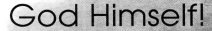

God Himself!

Mom: So, David, the next time a teacher or human expert says "Here's what happened in the past," you might just raise your hand and ask, politely of course, "Were you there?"

Dave: I get it, Mom. No human expert was there in the past to see where people came from, but God was. So we really ought to listen to the Word of God, not the words of men.

Dad: Right you are, Dave. And if someone asks you if you were there, you can just say, "No, I wasn't there, but I know Someone who was, and the answer's in Genesis, the first book in the Bible."

Dave: That's neat, Dad. But I still wonder about one thing. If evolution is not really science, why did I learn about it in science class?

Dad: Evolution uses lots of big words to describe living things like we use in life science (biology), and lots of big words about rocks and fossils like we use in earth science (geology).

Mom: And evolution believers want people to believe evolution is science, because scientists have discovered many wonderful things about our world.

Dave: Our teacher said the goal of science is to understand how our world works, and to use that knowledge to help people, as in exploring the moon and finding cures for diseases.

Dad: Your teacher is right Dave. I'm a scientist, and I love science. In fact, I think science is the friend of the Christian faith in its fight with evolution.

Dave: What do you mean, Dad?

Dad: Well, every time an evolution believer makes up a story about some bits and pieces of fossil bone . . .

Dave: . . . I get it! Every time an evolution believer makes up a story about the past, science shows his so-called evidence is just *man, ape, fake,* or *mistake!*

Dad: Right you are, Dave. Science showed us that Neanderthal "cave men," Blacks, and Bushmen are just people; that Rama and "Nutcracker Man" are just apes; that "Piltdown Man" was a fake that fooled the experts; and that "Java man" and "Nebraska Man" were huge mistakes!

Mom: In fact, David, what's the one thing we can say for sure about the so-called missing links?

Dave: I guess the one thing we can say for sure is that **the missing links are still missing**!

Dad: And I think the missing links will *always* be missing.

Dave: I think so, too, Dad. After all, the Bible says in Genesis that God created people and all the different animals separate in the beginning, and told them to "multiply after their kinds."

Mom: Science and Scripture agree. Man and apes have always been separate kinds. What we see in God's world agrees with what we read in God's Word, the Bible.

SCIENCE SCOREBOARD		
	Evolution Believers	Bible Believers
1. Neanderthals	Ape-man X	People ✓
2. African Blacks	Sub-human X	People ✓
3. Australian Bushmen	Sub-human X	People ✓
4. Piltdown Man	'Missing link' X	Fake ✓
5. Java Man	Ape-man X	Mistake ✓
6. Nutcracker Man	Man's ancestor X	Man's meal ✓
7. Nebraska	Ape-man X	Pig's tooth ✓
8. Rama	Upright ape X	Just ape ✓
	0	8

CHAPTER 4
DIG DEEPER!

People who believe in human evolution have certainly made lots of tragic mistakes and big scientific blunders in the past. But people who don't believe God still have to believe that somehow apes changed into people anyway. So, they just keep digging, hoping someday to find a missing link.

When all the evidence they once used proved wrong, believers in evolution turned their attention to a group of fossil skeletons in Africa. Publicity about these fossils made the Leaky family and Donald Johanson famous.

But what did they really find? Skeletons of ape-men? Or just apes and men? Or more fakes and mistakes? As part of her science project at school, our eldest daughter, Dana, asked us about those African fossils. Let's see what we found.

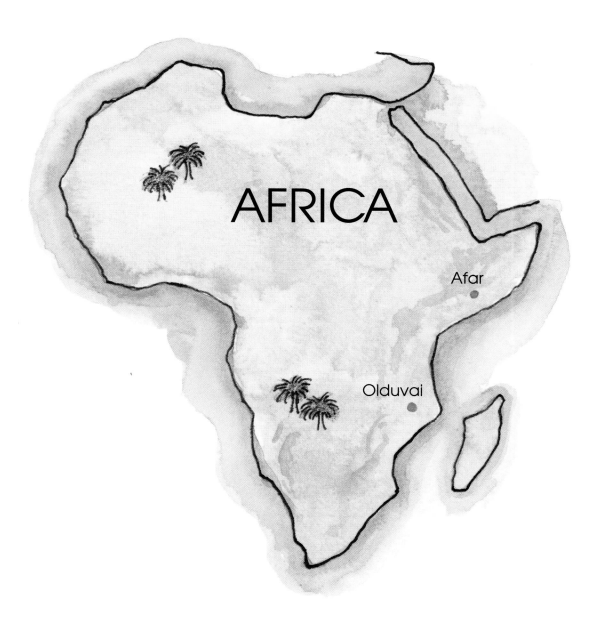

Dana: You're right about one thing, Dad. All those skeletons once used to prove evolution proved evolution wrong instead! My teacher agreed with you when I told him what you said about those fossils.

Dad: I'm glad to hear that, Dana.

Dana: Well, you may not be glad to hear the next part. My teacher also said that some new fossils have been discovered since then, and these new skeletons prove evolution after all. Sorry, Dad, I forgot what he called them.

Dad: Australopithecus (Aws TRALL oh PITH ee cuss)?

Dana: Yes, that's it! How did you know?

Dad: Remember, Dana, I'm a scientist who spends a lot of time studying fossils. It's my business to know things like that. "Australo — " means "southern." The first fossils in this group were apes found in southern Africa. "Australopicthecus" means "southern apes."

Dana: I wish we could go to Africa and dig out the bones first hand!

Dad: We can — in our imaginations.

JUMP INTO YOUR IMAGINATION AND JOIN US!

Dad: Here we are in Ethiopia. That's where Donald Johanson's team found bits and pieces of bone and put them together to make the famous *Australopithecus* called Lucy.

LUCY

Reconstruction of Lucy

Dana: Hmmm, Dad, Lucy is not just a tooth or a few bones. It looks like someone found most of a skeleton, almost everything but the head and feet.

Dad: Lucy does look like a pretty exciting discovery. The skeleton is about 40% complete.

Dana: Well, Dad, what about Lucy? Did evolution believers finally find a real missing link — a fossil part ape and part human? It looks like they found enough evidence this time to tell what Lucy really was.

Dad: We do have a lot of information about Lucy, Dana. In fact, we have so much information, we can be sure Johanson and his followers are **wrong** about what Lucy means!

Dana: Okay, Dad, tell me more!

Dad: First of all, everything about Lucy's skeleton is very, very ape-like. Johanson even said that Lucy was the ancestor of all the apes as well as human beings.

Dana: Why did he think Lucy was part human?

Mom: Because, he said, it walked upright — on two legs.

Dana: If Lucy did walk upright, would that make it part ape, part human?

Dad: Not really, Dana. There is an ape today that does a fair job of walking upright part of the time. It's the rain forest chimpanzee (*Pan paniscus*). Remember when I took pictures of them at the San Diego Zoo?

Dana: Oh yes. They were cute. And they weren't too bad at walking upright either.

Mom: Think about this, Dana: Everything else about Lucy is very ape-like. She walked no more upright than the living rain forest chimpanzee.

Dana: It sounds to me like Donald Johanson found the ancestor of chimpanzees, not of human beings!

Dad: You know what? Several leading scientists agree with us about Lucy. They still believe in evolution for other reasons, but they think Lucy is **not** a link between apes and people.

Dana: That's great, Dad. I wish we could hear what these other scientists say. At school all we ever hear is just one side of the story about a fossil, the evolution side.

Mom: I'm afraid you're right, Dana. And it's usually the things you're *not* told about a fossil that make it fit better with the Bible than with evolution.

Dad: Consider this, Dana. Johanson discovered Lucy and other pieces of fossil bone called "First Family" back in 1974. But it was seven years before other scientists were allowed to look at the bones and decide for themselves what the fossils really were.

LUCY
Link
between
apes
and man

D. Johanson

Dana: Meantime, I guess the news stories made a lot of people believe Johanson's ideas were right — even before those ideas were tested in a scientific way.

Dad: Right, Dana. I heard Johanson speak and show his slides myself. It was a good adventure story and fund raiser, but it seemed to have lots and lots of scientific weak spots. And other scientists see those weak spots, too.

Mom: For instance, when Johanson looked at the knee, he thought Lucy walked upright. But other scientists didn't just look; they took measurements.

Dana: What did the measurements show?

Mom: They showed that Lucy did **not** walk upright. In fact, another ape, an orangutan, would have walked more like a person than Lucy could.

Dana: I've seen orangutans at the zoo. They're cute and fun to watch, but they're just apes — not half ape, half person!

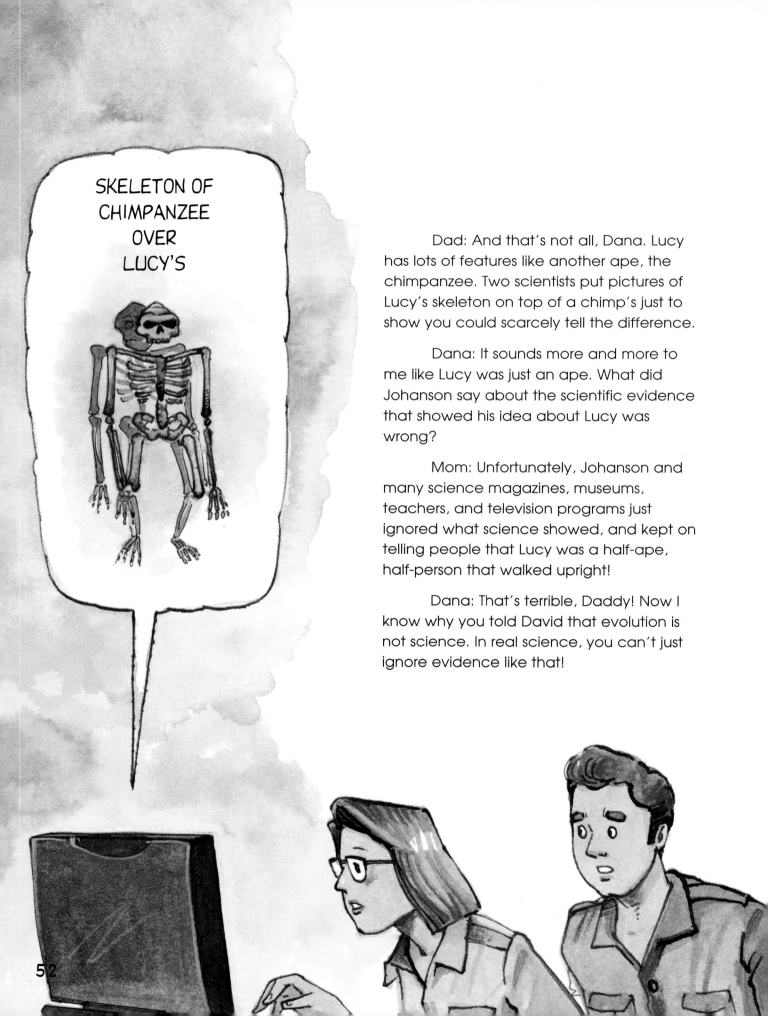

Dad: And that's not all, Dana. Lucy has lots of features like another ape, the chimpanzee. Two scientists put pictures of Lucy's skeleton on top of a chimp's just to show you could scarcely tell the difference.

Dana: It sounds more and more to me like Lucy was just an ape. What did Johanson say about the scientific evidence that showed his idea about Lucy was wrong?

Mom: Unfortunately, Johanson and many science magazines, museums, teachers, and television programs just ignored what science showed, and kept on telling people that Lucy was a half-ape, half-person that walked upright!

Dana: That's terrible, Daddy! Now I know why you told David that evolution is not science. In real science, you can't just ignore evidence like that!

Is this the way science should work?

Dad: And that's not the worst of it. Johanson said at first that Lucy's hip bone also showed it walked upright.

Mom: Then, when your Dad was speaking in New Zealand, we saw Johanson's TV program about Lucy. After 20 years, Johanson finally admitted that the hip bone made it hard to believe Lucy walked on two legs.

Dana: Oh? What did he say about that?

Dad: That's the sad part. He said there was something wrong with the fossil, not his idea. So — right on TV — he had someone saw the hip bone into pieces and glue it back together again. Then he said the cut-and-glued hip showed Lucy walked upright after all!

Dana: What?! That's not bad science; that's not science at all! That's just making up evidence to support what you want to believe!

Dad: A review in a New Zealand newspaper said just about the same thing, Dana. The writer said Johanson must think TV watchers are easy to fool, but he thought people had higher standards for scientific evidence than that!

Dana: Me, too, Dad. It looks like science proved evolution wrong once again.

Mom: Actually, Dana, Lucy and the other "southern apes" (*Australopithecus*) seem to be just apes, not very different from those living today. Their fossils are found with those of other African animals, just like living apes are found with giraffes, rhinos, snakes, guinea hens, and lots of hoofed animals today.

Dana: Come to think of it, it seems that these so-called "ape men" were found where apes live. And, if they're not fakes or mistakes, they usually turn out to be just apes after all.

Mom: That's right, Dana. And there is another important lesson here. Looking at **all** the evidence, and learning to make decisions — that's what good science and good education is all about!

Dad: Sadly, some schools teach only evolution and won't even let students talk about the evidence for creation. That's just prejudice and censorship — bad science and bad education.

Dana: I know what you mean, Dad. Sometimes evolution believers are so unsure of themselves that they get nervous or mad if a student even mentions the Bible.

Mom: The Bible tells us to study, and to be able to "give a reason" for our hope in God (I Peter 3:15). It's important to know not only what you believe, but why you believe it!

COULD FLESH
BE MILLIONS OF
YEARS OLD?

Dana: That makes me wonder about one thing. Why do evolution believers always say fossils of apes and people are millions of years old?

Mom: Not because of the scientific evidence, that's for sure. In his book, *The Young Earth*[4], a friend of ours, Dr. John Morris, shows there is a lot of evidence that fossils are only thousands of years old, many buried rapidly during Noah's flood and the violent catastrophes right after it.

Dad: Your mom once found a clam that evolution believers claim would be 10-25 million years old — but it still had some flesh on it!

Dana: That flesh would surely rot away in a lot less than one million years! What do evolution believers say about that?!

Dad: We took the clam to experts. They admitted her discovery was a real mystery for evolution — then showed us more "ancient" clams with flesh, making the mystery for evolution even worse!

Mom: Discoveries of dinosaur DNA and of fresh dinosaur bones by our friend, Buddy Davis, and his team, show that even dinosaurs lived only thousands of years ago, not millions.

Dana: There surely is a lot of evidence that evolution is wrong about human beginnings. Is there any evidence that can help people see the Bible is right?

Idea based on Bible:

Most fossils were formed

as stages of burial

during the year

of Noah's Flood

and

some human fossils

could be found

below apes.

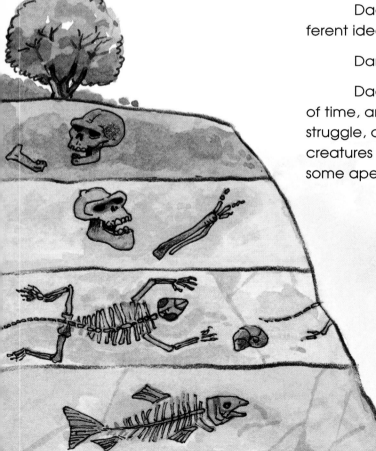

Dad: I think so, Dana. Suppose we found fossil human skeletons buried in rocks below the layers where Lucy was found. That would be bad for people who believe in evolution. But even better, it would be great for people who believe in the Bible.

Dana: Oh? Why do you say that, Dad?

Dad: Well, the Bible tells us that man and land animals were all created on the same day, Day Six of the Creation Week. That was before man's sin brought death into God's perfect world.

Mom: Since fossils are dead things, they must have been buried after sin ruined God's perfect creation. In fact . . .

Dana: In fact, most fossils are probably dead things buried in rock layers laid down by water all over the earth during Noah's Flood and right after!

Mom: Very good, Dana! And the different rock layers were formed very quickly — a lot of water, and a little bit of time.

Dad: People who believe in evolution have a much different idea about how rock layers form.

Dana: Oh? What do they believe?

Dad: They believe that rock layers formed slowly — a lot of time, and a little bit of water. They believe that time, chance, struggle, and death — evolution — slowly changed some sea creatures into land animals, some land animals into apes, and some apes into people.

Mom: So, Dana, if evolution were true, could you ever find the fossil of a human being in a rock layer below one where apes are first found?

Dana: I guess not. Evolution believers would have to say there were no people in the world to fossilize until after the apes came along to turn into people.

Dad: Exactly, Dana. But since the Bible is true, could you ever find human fossils below the deepest ape fossils?

Dana: Hmmm. Yes, I think you could. Man and apes were created at the same time and lived together before Noah's flood. So, even if they lived in different places and people were usually buried last, sometimes you could find a human fossil below the deepest ape.

Mom: Excellent, Dana. So if fossils of people are found in rock layers below those where apes and so-called "ape-men" are found, we have evidence that shows . . .

Dana: We have evidence that shows evolution is wrong and the Bible is right!

Dad: More accurately, the evidence would show that the view of evolution is wrong and would encourage those scientists who believe the Bible.

Idea based on evolution:

Fossils were formed
as stages of evolution
over millions of years
and
no human fossils
could be found
below apes.

Dana: Okay. So tell me, have we ever found fossils that support the Bible — fossils of people found deeper than apes, *before* any so-called ape-men like Lucy were buried?

Dad: Well, let's see. Let's travel back to a rock ledge near Laetoli (Lie tole ee) in Africa. What do you see?

Dana: It looks like a line of footprints in rock.

Mom: What kind of footprints?

Dana: Human, I guess. Even my foot fits into the print.

Mom: Do they look like ordinary human footprints?

Dana: Pretty much so, except they're sort of small and the steps are close together. But all people start small, and anybody can take short steps. What's so special about these footprints?

Mom: For one thing, Mary Leakey found them. Here's a picture similar to one in *National Geographic* that shows the kind of foot that she thinks made the prints.

Dana: See. That's just an ordinary foot, like yours or mine. What's the big deal? Where were these prints found, anyway?

Mom: That's the best part, Dana. They were found in a layer of fossil rock *below* the one where Lucy was found.

Dana: Now I get it! That means there's no way at all Lucy could be a link between ape and man!

Mom: Why not?

Dana: Lucy couldn't be the ancestor of people if people were already walking around before Lucy was turned into a fossil! The footprints Mary Leakey found really support what the Bible says!

Dad: I agree, Dana. But you might be surprised at what Mary Leakey once had an artist draw on top of those feet. Take a look at this picture.

Dana: What's that a picture of? Man? Ape? Ape-man?

Dad: The picture is supposed to be a sort of ape-man. I admire Mary Leakey and her dedication to her work very much, but I think it's much more logical and scientific to think that human beings are the ones who make human footprints.

Dana: What do other scientists say?

Dad: After lots of work on the tracks, one scientist said he had "shocking" and "disturbing" news.

Dana: What was that?

Dad: He tried very hard to prove that the tracks Mary Leakey found near Laetoli were made by some kind of animal and not by human beings. He even studied the tracks made in mud by a dancing bear! But, after long study, he came to the same conclusion you and I did: you can't tell the difference between the tracks Mary Leakey found and ordinary human tracks.

Dana: That sounds great to me! Why did he call it "shocking" and "disturbing?"

Dad: It's great news if you believe the Bible, Dana. But it's "shocking" and "disturbing" news for evolution. It means they have no evidence left at all for human evolution. They have to start over again looking for missing links, looking below the level where Mary Leakey found those human tracks.

Dana: Hurray for our side! But . . . could those tracks have been made by apes?

Dad: No. Apes have something like "four hands." Their feet have a big toe that acts like our thumb, so their footprint is very different from ours. Bear tracks are closer to ours, but their track is short and stubby. It has no arch, and the toes have big claws.

Mom: Here's some good news, Dana. Mary Leakey once thought the tracks she discovered might belong to an ape-man, like that picture we showed you. But now it seems she has changed her mind. In her son's television series, she just called them human tracks.

Dana: That's great, Mom! It sounds to me like the evidence that supports the Bible is just getting better all the time — even the evidence discovered by scientists who believe in evolution!

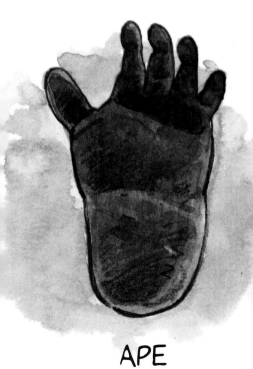

APE

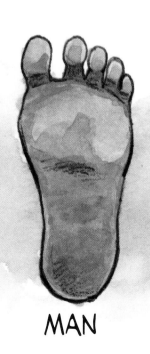

MAN

BEAR

Dad: Well put, Dana. In fact, Mary Leakey's son, Richard, recently found some more evidence that encourages Christians: a fossil skeleton so well preserved, scientists could tell it was a boy about 12 years old.

Dana: That's neat, Dad, but how does that support the Bible?

Dad: The skeleton was like that of a modern human, *Homo sapiens*, in every way, but it was buried so deep that Richard Leakey wanted to call it something less than the modern man, *Homo erectus*. But that would be a scientific mistake.

Mom: At a university talk, your father explained to an evolution expert that everything about the boy, even the boy's brain size, was fully human, and the man just said, "Oh, you're right about that."

Dana: Wow, Dad! Tell me more! Is there more evidence of man buried before man's so-called ancestors?

Dad: Yes, Dana lots of evidence. It's possible that a few people got buried early in Noah's flood, and there are reports of their fossil skeletons and tools in coal and other rock layers that would put man way before apes, at least according to evolution beliefs about rock layers.

Dana: Come to think of it, the evidence I read in *The Great Dinosaur Mystery*[5] about man and dinosaurs living together would surely surprise evolution believers!

Mom: Evolution believers ignore some of these out-of-place fossils because they weren't discovered by scientists, but they can't say that about Casteinedolo (KAS tein ee DOE lo) Man.

Dad: Several human fossils were found by a scientist in rock layers far below those with any so-called ape-men. A famous expert said the Casteinedolo discovery would shatter his belief in evolution — but he kept on believing in evolution anyway.

Dana: With all the evidence against it, why does anyone believe the ape-man story of evolution?

Dad: Sad to say, Dana, several famous experts have said they believe in evolution just because they don't want to believe in God.

Dana: That is sad, Dad. That's almost like believing a lie when you know what the truth really is.

Mom: *Creation* magazine told about a famous zoo, Dana, that put a model of Johanson's Lucy in the human footprints Mary Leakey found in Laetoli[6].

Dana: That's not right, Mom. Those fossils were found in different parts of Africa, and the Lucy skeleton didn't even have any feet!

Mom: The "experts" at the zoo admitted their display didn't show the real facts, but they wouldn't change it because it taught evolution.

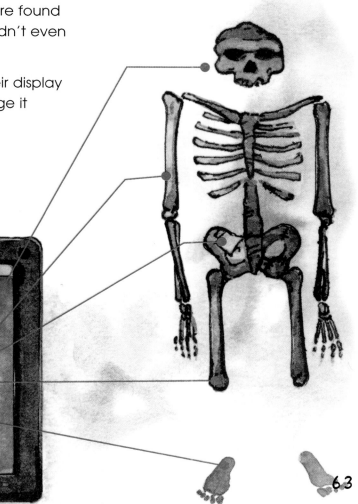

Lucy -
missing link
or
mixed-up mistake

Skull - from imagination
Bone - like chimp from afar
Pelvis - cut and glued
Knee - less human than
          Orang-utan
Foot   - human foot print
          from Laetoli

63

Dana: That's terrible! You mean they would rather tell the story of evolution than tell the truth about fossils?!

Mom: Certainly the fossils found so far make it hard to believe in evolution and easy to believe what the Bible says about a perfect world created by God, ruined by man, destroyed by Noah's flood, and restored to new life in Jesus Christ — creation, corruption, catastrophe, Christ!

Dana: That's neat! But, I sometimes wonder about the future. Do you think people who believe in evolution will ever find a real missing link?

Dad: I know this, Dana. If you hear about some "new discovery" in the news, wait until <u>all</u> the evidence is in before you decide. And expect to wait a few years, too, so other scientists can study the evidence.

Mom: People's ideas are always changing. When it comes to human beginnings, what's "fact" one day may be "false" the next. Thank goodness, God's Word never changeS!

Dana: It certainly makes more sense to believe the never-changing Word of God than the ever-changing words of men!

Dad: I agree, Dana. I've written five science textbooks, but I've had to re-write them all to bring them up-to-date. God never had to re-write the Bible once; God got it right the first time!

The Ever Changing Words of Man

The Never Changing Word of God

Which has told us the truth about the past?
Which should we trust to tell us about the future?

Mom: In the Bible, God tells us the truth about our past, present, and future!

Dad: I'm a scientist, and you know I love science, Dana. Science works great in the present, but science has no way to study the past or the future.

Mom: No person knows everything, so everyone must really live by faith.

Dana: But God knows everything. And faith in **God's Word, the Bible, is a faith that fits the facts. Evolution is a faith the facts have failed**.

Mom: That's an excellent summary, Dana. And if you want to know what the future holds, you have to know the One who holds the future.

Dana: What do evolution believers think about the future?

Dad: According to evolution, human beings will finally die out or become extinct. Death wins.

Dana: But according to the Bible, life wins — the new life we can have in Jesus Christ, and life forever in heaven with Him!

Dad: Amen, Dana. "Even so, come Lord Jesus."

CHAPTER 5
IN GOD'S IMAGE

I hope you've enjoyed looking with our family at all the fossil "skeletons in our closet." All these bones tell us that evolution is completely wrong about human beginnings. They also support what the Bible says, that God created people and animals separately, each "after their own kinds" (Genesis 1).

But the Bible tells us more than just *that* God created us. It also tells us *how* he did it. God did **not** create people from an animal using the trial-and-error method of evolution — time, chance, struggle, and death. Instead, God created the first person supernaturally from the "dust of the ground," and He made us "in His image." To find out more about what that means, join the conversation with our youngest daughter, Diane.

Di: I like how all those fossils show that God created. That makes each person something special.

Mom: That's right, Diane. Each person — and that means YOU — has a special place in God's plan.

Di: But how did God do it? How did He make the very first person?

Dad: What's that on the table over there, Diane?

Di: It's a fruit bowl. It's the one I made in arts and crafts at Bible school today.

Dad: What did you use to make your fruit bowl, Diane?

Di: I used some clay the teacher gave me. I shaped the clay with my hands. Then the teacher put it in the oven to make it hard. After that, I got to paint it.

Dad: Guess what, Diane. I think the way you made that fruit bowl helps us understand how God made people.

Di: Really? How can that be?

Dad: The Bible says that the first person, Adam, was created from the "dust of the ground." That means God used simple materials, sort of like your lump of clay, to create people.

Mom: In fact, the Bible says, "God is the Potter; we are the clay" (Isaiah 64:8).

Di: That's neat, Mom and Dad! So, when I shaped my bowl of clay, I sort of copied what God did when He made people. Is that what you mean?

Dad: In a way, it is Diane. But there are also lots of differences between your creation and God's creation. You could harden your clay bowl and paint it, but God could do more. He could breathe life into His creation!

Di: Wow! But that makes me wonder. When God breathed life into Adam, could Adam walk and talk, or did he have to slowly learn how to do those things?

Mom: Look at your computer over there, Diane. When we got you the voice machine for it and first plugged it in, did it start off by grunting and then slowly learn how to talk?

Di: Of course not, Mom! Just as soon as we gave it power, it started talking — using big words and everything!

Dad: If computer experts can use materials out of the ground to make machines that talk, then . . .

Di: Then it would be easy for God to make Adam out of the dust of the ground so that he could talk, big words and all!

Mom: In fact, the Bible tells us (Genesis) that God talked daily with Adam and Even while they were in the Garden of Eden.

Di: That would be great, Mom. I wonder what they talked about?

Dad: Adam and Eve didn't have to learn how to talk, but they did have lots of things to learn about taking care of their beautiful home, the Earth, that God had given them. Maybe that's what they talked about.

Mom: And, of course, God created Adam and Eve as adults that could walk and run without having to learn how to crawl first.

Di: The computer robot the Waldens showed us could walk and do all sorts of motions, and it was just created by people. So it would be really easy for God to create people that could walk and talk and do all sorts of things, just the way God designed them ahead of time.

Mom: I think it's even possible that Adam and Eve could write.

Dad: The Bible mentions "the book of Adam." Maybe it was a book *by* Adam, not just a book *about* Adam.

Di: Well, when we hook my computer into the printer, it writes. My computer can even spell big words I can't even spell yet. I guess if people can program a computer to write, God could program Adam and Eve to write!

Mom: Maybe our first parents could even write poetry. The first poem in the Bible is Adam's response to God's creation of Eve to be Adam's wife.

Di: So the first poem was about a girl. That's neat, Mom!

Mom: Eve is special in another way, Diane. Adam and the land plants and animals were just made out of the dust of the ground, but Eve was made from a part of Adam's side.

Dad: Our first parents were given a big job, too. God put Adam and Eve in charge of taking care of the whole Earth, keeping it a Garden of Delight (Eden), as God had given it to them (Genesis 2:15; 1:28-30).

Di: Wow! One thing is for sure: people didn't start off as grunting four-legged animals that slowly learned how to talk and walk, like evolution believers say. The very first people were created smart and talented, better than any computer or robot man ever made!

Dad: Right you are, Diane. In fact, the Bible tells us that the children and grandchildren of Adam and Eve could grow crops, keep animals, make musical instruments, shape metal, and build cities (Genesis 4)!

Mom: As your Dad told Dave, even people living today in simple cultures, falsely called "Stone Age," are smart and talented. And records of ancient peoples show evidence of fully human abilities in art, science, business, and technology.

Dad: The evidence is crystal clear, there never were any half ape-half people that could only grunt and shuffle along. Science shows us evolution is wrong, and supports what the Bible says about mankind created "in the image of God" (Genesis 1:27).

71

TALKING

WRITING

CREATING

Di: Hmm. God created people "in His image." Does that mean we look like God?

Dad: No. It's not the way we *look* that makes us like God. Instead, it's more the things we *do*. We were created "in His image" so we could do things somewhat like God does.

Mom: God creates things, and, like a reflection of God, so do we. God loves, and so do we.

Dad: Of course, we don't do things as well as God does. But still, the way we create, love, work with a purpose, and even think about forever — all these are things we *do* which make us, in a small way, like the God who created us.

Di: Wow! I guess those things do make people pretty special. There aren't any animals that do all those things like people do!

LOVING

Dad: That's right, Diane. But we do have some things in common with the animals God created, too.

Di: What do you mean, Dad?

Dad: Well, God also created the animals out of the ground. He used the same simple materials to make animals that He used to created our bodies.

Mom: And some animals have eyes and ears and legs, like people do. And they have bones and muscles and blood on the inside, too.

Di: Come to think of it, some monkeys do look sort of like people!

Mom: Sometimes we may think so, but our feet are more like a bear's, and so is our diet. Human milk is more like a donkey's!

Dad: When it comes to the way we talk, people are more like dolphins or even parrots than apes or monkeys. Apes can be taught to type, but not to make talking sounds like other animals and people can.

Di: You make it sound like people are all "mixed up," Dad.

Dad: In a way we are, Diane. Different parts of the human body remind us of different animals, not always apes or monkeys. That's why scientists will use one kind of animal to study the foods we eat, a different animal to see if chemicals are safe to use, and still another animal to study the way we fight disease.

Di: I think I understand. Some things about the way we act make us like God. And some parts of our bodies remind us of the different animals God made.

Mom: It's really our spirits that make us most like God, Diane. God is a Spirit, and God created each person with a spirit, too — a spirit that lives on even after our bodies die!

Dad: So, Diane, each person is really body, soul, and spirit — partly like other creatures made by God, and partly like God Himself, our Creator!

Di: That's neat! When we die, do our spirits go to be with God in heaven?

Mom: If we believe in Jesus, they do, Diane.

Dad: And in heaven, God gives each spirit a new body, a perfect body, that will never die!

Di: Well, God did make the first person out of the ground. So, I guess it would be easy for God to make us new bodies in heaven.

Dad: Right you are, Sweetheart.

Mom: While He was on earth, Jesus even showed us how He could raise people from the dead.

Di: I remember, Mom. One man died, and he was buried in a cave for three days. But when Jesus called his name, he walked right out of his grave!

Dad: That was Lazarus (LAZ ah russ), Diane. And you're right — except he sort of had to hobble out of his grave, because he was all wrapped up in the bandages used to bury people in those days.

Mom: The story of Lazarus also shows that it doesn't take long for God to create life. Jesus just spoke and Lazarus' dead body came to life that instant. And when Christ comes again, our bodies will be changed "in the twinkling of an eye!"

Dad: As a scientist, I can tell you it would be harder to bring life to a dead body than to build a person from fresh material. But God in Christ is so powerful, all He had to do was speak, and it happened!

Di: I'm glad Jesus is so powerful. That means He can take care of me no matter what happens. Even when I die, He can give me a new body that will never die again!

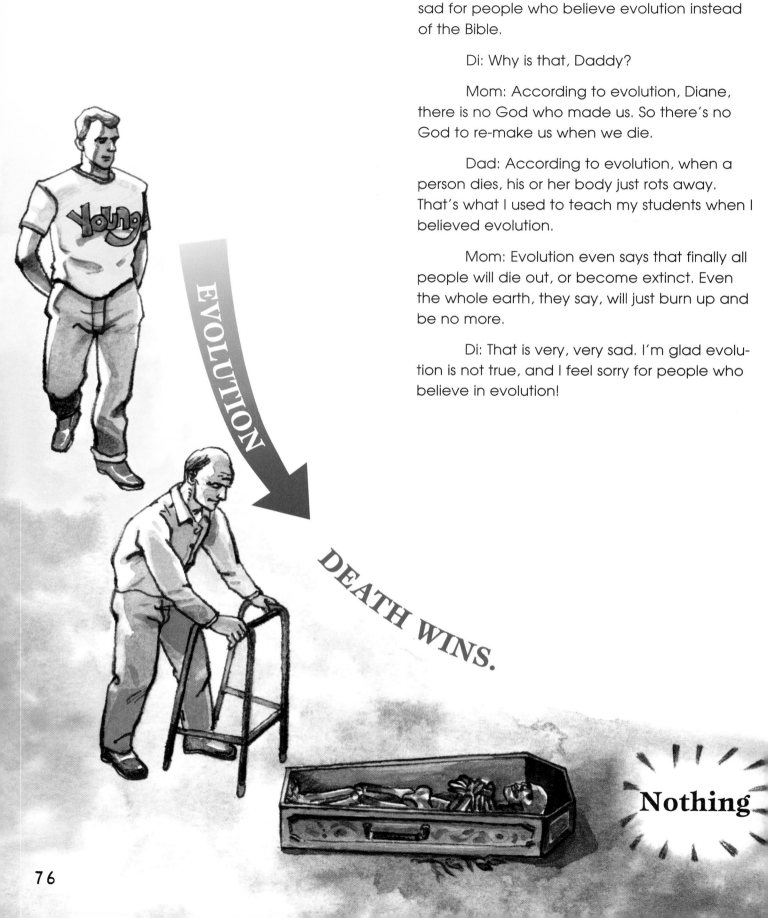

Dad: That's right, Diane. But it makes me sad for people who believe evolution instead of the Bible.

Di: Why is that, Daddy?

Mom: According to evolution, Diane, there is no God who made us. So there's no God to re-make us when we die.

Dad: According to evolution, when a person dies, his or her body just rots away. That's what I used to teach my students when I believed evolution.

Mom: Evolution even says that finally all people will die out, or become extinct. Even the whole earth, they say, will just burn up and be no more.

Di: That is very, very sad. I'm glad evolution is not true, and I feel sorry for people who believe in evolution!

EVOLUTION

DEATH WINS.

Nothing

Dad: Me, too, Diane. It's such a joy to know that God, our Creator, is also the One who can make us a "new creation in Christ." He can even raise our bodies to live with him in the "new heavens and new earth" where peace and joy go on forever!

Di: I guess that's why the Bible is called "good news." Living forever with Jesus is really good news!

Mom: That's for sure, Diane.

Dad: And everything we truly learn in God's world helps us to believe God's Word.

Di: Thanks, Mom and Dad. I'm going to ask God to help me tell others about Jesus, so they can live forever with Him, too.

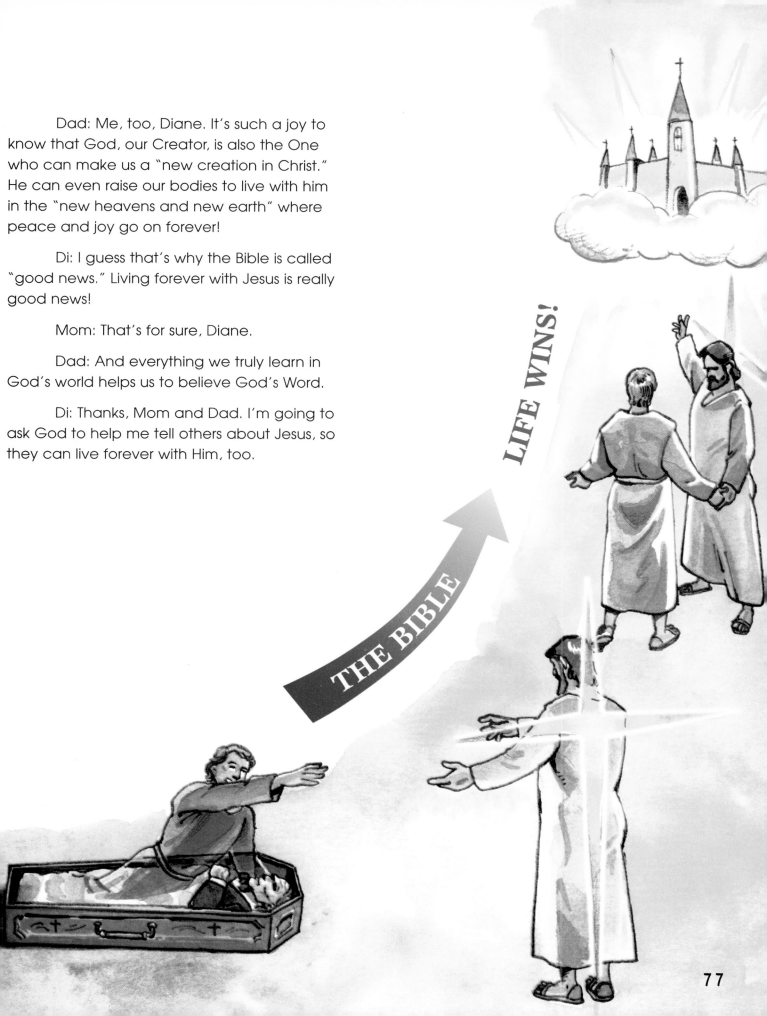

THE BIBLE

LIFE WINS!

ENDNOTES

[1] Doolan, R. & Wieland, C. 1995. "Filling in the blanks", *Creation*, Vol. 17(2), March-May, p.16-18.

[2] Weston, P. 1997. "Camels: Confirmation of Creation", *Creation*, Vol. 19(4), September-November, p.26-29.

[3] MacLeish, K. 1972. "The Tasadays: Stone Age Cavemen of Mindanao", *National Geographic*, August, p.218-249.

[4] Taylor, I. 1986. "National Geographic and the Stone Age Swindle?", *Creation*, Vol. 9(1), December, p.6-10.

[5] Morris, J. 1994. <u>The Young Earth</u>. Master Books, Green Forest, Arkansas.

[6] Taylor, P. 1987. <u>The Great Dinosaur Mystery and the Bible</u>. Chariot Victor Publ., Colorado Springs, Colorado.

[7] Staff Editor. 1997. "Ape-woman' Statue Misleads Public: Anatomy Professor", *Creation*, 19(1), December 1996-February 1997, p.52.

ADDITIONAL BOOKS BY AUTHOR GARY PARKER

• *Dry Bones and Other Fossils*
A full-color book for elementary-age children, presenting evidence for Noah's flood, how fossils are formed, found, and displayed.
$12.95, Hardcover, 80 pages, ISBN: 0-89051-203-5

• *Life Before Birth*
A tasteful, educational treatment of the reproduction process, especially written for parents struggling to explain this miracle to children.
$12.95, Hardcover, 88 pages, ISBN: 0-89051-164-0

• *Creation Facts of Life*
Examines the classic arguments for evolution, as taught in public schools and universities, then refutes them in an easy-to-read style.
$9.95, Paperback, 176 pages, ISBN: 0-89051-200-0

• *What is Creation Science?*
(written with Dr. Henry Morris)
Two leading creation scientists provide conclusive evidence for intelligent design and critically examine the major arguments used to support evolution.
$11.95, Paperback, 336 pages, ISBN: 0-89051-081-4

These books are available through your local Christian bookstore, or write to:
Master Books, P.O. Box 727, Green Forest, Arkansas, 72638

By James Howe • Illustrated by Sakika Kikuchi

MILO WALKING

Abrams Books for Young Readers • New York

Every morning, Milo goes
walking with his mother.

They take the same walk
around their neighborhood.
But what they see is never the same.

"Look, Mama, this puddle wasn't here yesterday."

"It rained during the night while you were sleeping."

Milo looks at the clouds in the puddle.

"The rain left this puddle for me to find," Milo says.

"Yes," says his mother.

Milo looks at the boy in the puddle
and touches his wet hands to the puddle boy's hands.

"We are meeting," Milo says. "Hello, Milo."

"Hello, Milo," his mother says in a wobbly voice.

"The boy in the puddle sounds funny," says Milo.

"He is under the water," says his mother.

"Goodbye, Milo," Milo says, splashing the puddle.
"Goodbye, clouds. Goodbye, puddle."

Milo and his mother walk on.

"Listen," says Milo. "There are bees."

"Don't they have a lot to say this morning?" his mother asks.
"How in the world do they get so much done when they
are talking all the time?"

"They know what they are doing," says Milo. "They don't have to
think about it."

"How smart of you," Milo's mother says. "And how smart of the bees."

Milo bends down to smell the yellow flowers.
"Sometimes you smell like these flowers,"
he tells his mother.

His mother smiles.

Milo loves all flowers, but these yellow flowers are his favorite.

"Oh, look!" Milo's mother says.

Up, up, Milo sees the cloud tail of a plane drifting
across the summer sky. He closes his eyes
and listens, but all he can hear are the bees.

And a woodpecker high up in a tree.

Milo loves birds almost as much as
he loves flowers. The woodpecker is
his favorite.

"I think that woodpecker has a red head,"
he tells his mother.

"And a coat that is speckled black and white.
Can you see it?"

"It is too far away," says Milo. "But if I close
my eyes, I can."

"Mmm," Milo's mother says.

They are quiet until they come to the bench,
where they sit every day and share a box of juice.

"'Speckled' is such a lovely word, isn't it?" his mother asks.

"It's fun to say," says Milo. "Speckled."

"Speckled," says his mother.

"The tree looks sad today," Milo says.

"Why do you think that?"

Milo does not have an answer.
He just knows that the tree looks sad.

When they are ready to walk again,
Milo hugs the tree and whispers,
"It's OK. I will see you tomorrow
and you will be happy."

Now Blue runs up to say hello to Milo. Blue is the big dog who lives one street over. She is full of slobber and good intentions.

"She can't help it," Milo says, laughing as he wipes slobber off his cheeks. "She loves us."

"She does," says his mother.

"Goodbye, Blue," Milo says.

Milo and his mother walk the rest of the way home
hand in hand, thinking their own thoughts.

When they get to their house, Milo turns back and says, "I wish we saw butterflies."

Milo loves flowers and birds, but more than anything, he loves butterflies.

"Maybe we will tomorrow," says his mother.

"Maybe," Milo says.

After having a snack, Milo says to his mother,
"I am going to write a story. If I tell you the words,
will you write them down? I will draw the pictures."

"Of course," his mother tells him. "Does the story have a title?"

"'Milo Walking,'" says Milo. "It begins with Milo looking in a puddle. Don't write that part."

"What should I write?"

"'Last night, when Milo was sleeping, the rain came down.'"

He waits for his mother to write down the words. Then he draws a puddle and says, "'The rain left a puddle for Milo to find.'"

Milo's mother writes, then rests her pencil as Milo thinks about what will happen next.

There will be bees and yellow flowers
and a plane and a speckled woodpecker.

There will be a sad tree
and a happy, slobbering dog.

And there will be butterflies.